THE ADVENTURES OF
HOOVER
THE FBI DOG

Hoover Travels the World

Joel Altman

illustrated by
Jon Chad

Hello, my name is Hoover, and as you can see, I am a Black Labrador Retriever. I am a proud member of the Federal Bureau of Investigation. I have an important job at the FBI, where I work as an Explosives Detection K-9. I was trained to help FBI Police officers detect explosives anywhere that they might need me. I can search trucks, cars, planes, schools, buildings, stadiums, open fields or just about anywhere else.

I trained for almost three months with my human partner, Joel. My reward for finding explosives is dog food that Joel gives me when I show him where explosives are hidden. I was originally trained to be a guide dog but my human friends thought that I would be a great explosives detector instead!

I've just been called to FBI Headquarters for a very important meeting.

I walk through the J. Edgar Hoover Building to the Office of the Director. "Come on in, Hoover," says the Director. As he hands me a piece of paper, he says that I've been selected for a very important assignment. My special assignment is to travel the world, searching for other working dogs and learning more about the types of jobs they have. I'm looking forward to seeing so many interesting places and sharing my experiences with other dogs!

"Are you up to the task?" asks the Director. I bark enthusiastically, YES!

My first stop is right here in Washington, D.C., our Nation's Capital. At the Washington Monument, I come across my first working dog, a Golden Retriever named Sandy. Golden Retrievers are very good at helping visually impaired people find their way around as guide dogs. I tell Sandy that I was originally a guide dog before I learned how to find explosives. Sandy can guide his human companion safely anywhere she needs to go by using a special harness and knowing when it is safe to walk.

From the Washington Monument, it was a quick walk to the White House, where I say hello to Bo the Portuguese Water Dog. His job is to keep our President and First Family happy. Bo likes to chase squirrels and walk around the grounds of the White House. Sometimes, he falls asleep in the Oval Office and dreams that he is the President!

Next, I continue to the United States Capitol Building, where I encounter an assistance dog named Dustin. Dustin is trained to be a companion for people with disabilities. He can do many things, like turn on lights, open doors and pick up things in his mouth to give to his human companion. Dustin was trained to know over forty commands. He goes everywhere with his human companion and they are the best of friends!

I continue to the Lincoln Memorial to play with a German Shepherd named Bak. He works for the Metropolitan Police Department in Washington, D.C. and he helps find illegal drugs that people try to hide. Bak says that he came from the Czech Republic and that he was specially bred to be a police dog. Instead of food, Bak's reward for finding drugs is a tennis ball that his human partner throws to him. Bak is very protective and will bark at people who come near. Bak says that when you see a working dog, you should always ask the handler's permission before you try to pet the dog.

Staying in Washington, D.C., I make my way to the Children's Hospital, where I meet a Great Dane named Wally and two Poodles named Benny and Beamer. These new friends are therapy dogs. People who are in the hospital enjoy friendly visits from dogs, especially gentle dogs like these new friends.

We make our way through the hospital spreading joy and hope from room to room. I love seeing so many smiles on the faces of children! We spend many hours at the hospital until we have visited everyone. Wally, Benny and Beamer tell me that they come to the hospital every week to visit those who are sick or recovering and can't leave their rooms.

From Washington, D.C., I'm off to nearby Quantico, Virginia and the FBI Academy. This is where FBI employees train for their various jobs. I hop into a helicopter and I fly deep into the woods to meet up with an FBI Bloodhound named Sadie. Bloodhounds have an amazing sense of smell and can help law enforcement in many ways.

Sadie is practicing finding the scent of a lost person and she is able to track that person down even after many hours or even days! Sadie tells me that she lives at the FBI Academy and leaves only when she is needed for an assignment. She enjoys her job because her only purpose is to find the scent of missing people and she loves to get outside and work!

Now it's time to leave the United States and travel the world! I board a jet and start the long journey across the Atlantic Ocean. In Europe, my first stop is Switzerland and the Swiss Alps. At a ski resort, I run into a St. Bernard named Hunter. Hunter is a very big dog! We play on the slopes and then he shows me how he is skilled at search and rescue. Hunter often helps find people buried in avalanches. Hunter and other rescue dogs can work without their human partners and can squeeze into very tight spaces. Sometimes, they even have small cameras mounted on them so that their handlers can see where they are inside of buildings. Some rescue dogs are even trained to swim to help people who might be drowning!

From Europe, I continue to the Middle East. In Iraq, I meet many brave American service men and women. I also meet a brave service dog, a Belgian Malinois named Lex. He looks funny because he is wearing a special vest and goggles, but both are important to keep him safe in the desert. Lex can do two jobs; he can search for explosives and he is also able to search for people that could be hiding from our troops.

Lex says that there are many U.S. Military working dogs all over the world who keep our country safe. Military dogs can work as watchdogs, as well as detect explosives and serve as mascots. Lex says that when he retires he wants to become a therapy dog and visit wounded veterans. I learned so much during my stay in Iraq, but now it's time to move on.

Next, I make the long journey to the South Atlantic Ocean and the tiny islands off the coast of Argentina known as the Falkland Islands. The Falkland Islands are known for producing wool for sweaters and other clothing. The sheep outnumber the people here by the thousands! With so many sheep, there are lots of herding dogs on the islands.

Herding dogs keep all of the sheep in order and make sure that they don't run away. I make friends with a Border Collie named Chloe, a Welsh Corgi named Barclay and a Belgian Tervuren named Isabel. It is cold here in the Falkland Islands, but I enjoy running over the rolling hills and I don't mind the temperature because I have a warm fur coat! These dogs do a great job of keeping the sheep going in the right direction. Baaaaaah!

From way south, I head north to the frozen tundra of the Arctic Circle in Alaska. Here, I run with a pack of Siberian Huskies and two Alaskan Malamutes named Callie and Bailey. Our musher guides us through the snow and ice. Callie tells me that these dogs can run for many hours at a time. Callie also says that some of these dogs were used by the first Antarctic explorers to help reach the South Pole over 100 years ago!

Bailey tells me that many years ago sled dogs helped the people of Alaska transport important things like supplies and mail. Now, sled dogs run a big sled race every year called the Iditarod to remember those times. The race is over 1,150 miles long across the snow and ice of Alaska! As I run along with these dogs, I get tired after a while, but they seem to be able to go...and go...and go!

Finally, it's back to Washington, D.C. and my home. At the airport, I meet up with a Beagle named Bosco, who is part of the Beagle Brigade. Beagles, with their keen sense of smell, are very good at searching through luggage at the airport for any food or animal products that may be coming into the country illegally. I think they also enjoy riding on the conveyor belts!

Beagles love to find things like food because they think with their stomachs all of the time and are always hungry! Since beagles are small they can move in and around people and luggage very easily. It sounds like Bosco and the Beagle Brigade have a very important task to do to keep our airports safe.

From the airport, I head straight back to FBI Headquarters to meet with the Director. "Mission accomplished!" I bark and the Director gives me a thumbs-up! I also tell all of my fellow FBI Police service dogs about my adventures.

My friends at work are Kurt, Power, Andy, Dora, Jamie, Darrell, Atwood and Shirley. They are all eager to know every detail of my travels. When we are not working, my K-9 friends and I live at home with our human handlers. Not only are we working dogs, we are also members of their families and we spend every day together. We are always ready to go to work and we train every day to keep people safe.

My last stop is my home where I am happy to be reunited with my little brother named Clifford. Clifford is a Hungarian Vizsla, a hunting dog. Some dogs like him are used to hunt birds, but Clifford is too silly to do anything like that! His job is just to be a pet and a brother for me. He is the fastest dog I know and loves to chase rabbits in the yard. We play... and play...and play!

The sun goes down and I am happy to be on my own bed after my amazing trip. Soon, I'm fast asleep, dreaming about my next FBI adventure. I can't wait to find out where I will go next!

This book is dedicated to the memory of FBI Hostage Rescue Team K-9 "Freddy" who lost his life in the line of duty. Freddy, a Belgian Malinois, was born in February 2007 and entered duty with the HRT in September 2008 as a tactical apprehension and explosives detection K-9. On October 28, 2009, Freddy's heroic actions saved the lives of his handler and fellow HRT teammates.

Joel Altman served as a member of the FBI Police and the Explosives K-9 unit at FBI Headquarters from 2004 to 2011. His K-9 partner, "Kurt", is a black Labrador retriever and was trained by the Bureau of Alcohol, Tobacco, Firearms and Explosives. Before becoming a police K-9, "Kurt" was originally trained as a guide dog for the blind by The Seeing Eye Inc. Joel and "Kurt" enjoy meeting young people and sharing what police K-9 teams do when they are working. Joel enjoys writing children's books about dogs in his free time.

You can read more about Kurt and the other FBI K-9s at:
http://www.fbi.gov/kids/dogs/chem/kurt/kurt.htm

Look out for Hoover's next big adventure...coming soon!